Male C
noisy

Male CRICKETS make
a chirping sound!

COCKROACHES
can eat almost anything!

DADDY LONGLEGS
do not make webs!

DRAGONFLIES can fly up to thirty miles per hour!

SUPER BUGS

BY MICHELLE MEADOWS · ILLUSTRATED BY BILL MAYER

ORCHARD BOOKS · NEW YORK · AN IMPRINT OF SCHOLASTIC INC.

AUTHOR'S NOTE

I have always been fascinated with bugs. There is something about them being so tiny in a big world. For a bug, there are so many dangers — like getting slurped up by bigger creatures or squashed by people. I've always thought that bugs are a beautiful part of nature, and I have fond memories of catching lightning bugs when I was a little girl. I wanted to create a book with a world where superhero bugs protect other insects from danger.

We tend to think of all creepy-crawly creatures as bugs. But through research, I discovered that not all insects are "true bugs" in the scientific sense. So I set out to identify the difference between true bugs and other insects. All bugs are insects, but not all insects are bugs. True bugs are a type of insect in the class Insecta and the scientific order Hemiptera, and they have a piercing or sucking mouthpart called a *proboscis*.

I was surprised to learn that spiders and daddy longlegs are not insects. Insects have six legs. Spiders and daddy longlegs are arachnids with eight legs.

A NOTE ABOUT THE ARTWORK

You might be surprised to find out that Bill Mayer paints in miniature. In fact, the Super Bugs are actually about the size of a thumbnail! Once the miniature paintings are finished, Bill scans them to create a digital file, and then the paintings are enlarged to fit the size of the book now in your hands. Bill painted *Super Bugs* using gouache, a paint containing more opaque pigments than watercolor, which makes for a richer color palette.

Text copyright © 2016 by Michelle Meadows
Illustrations copyright © 2016 by Bill Mayer

Library of Congress Cataloging-in-Publication Number: 2015027276
ISBN 978-0-545-68756-0
10 9 8 7 6 5 4 3 2 1   16 17 18 19 20

Printed in Malaysia 108
First edition, July 2016
The display and text type was set in Gotham.
Book design by Charles Kreloff and David Saylor

For Crystal Rice, Bridget Henig, and Mandy Eisemann — M.M.

For my best buddy, Forest, who bugs me every day — B.M.

Antennae up, eyes down.
Buzzing all around the town.

Super Bugs, Super Bugs, mighty, mighty Super Bugs!

Fast and fit, super strong.

Helping insects all day long.

Duty calls, busting walls.

Catch a stinkbug when she falls.

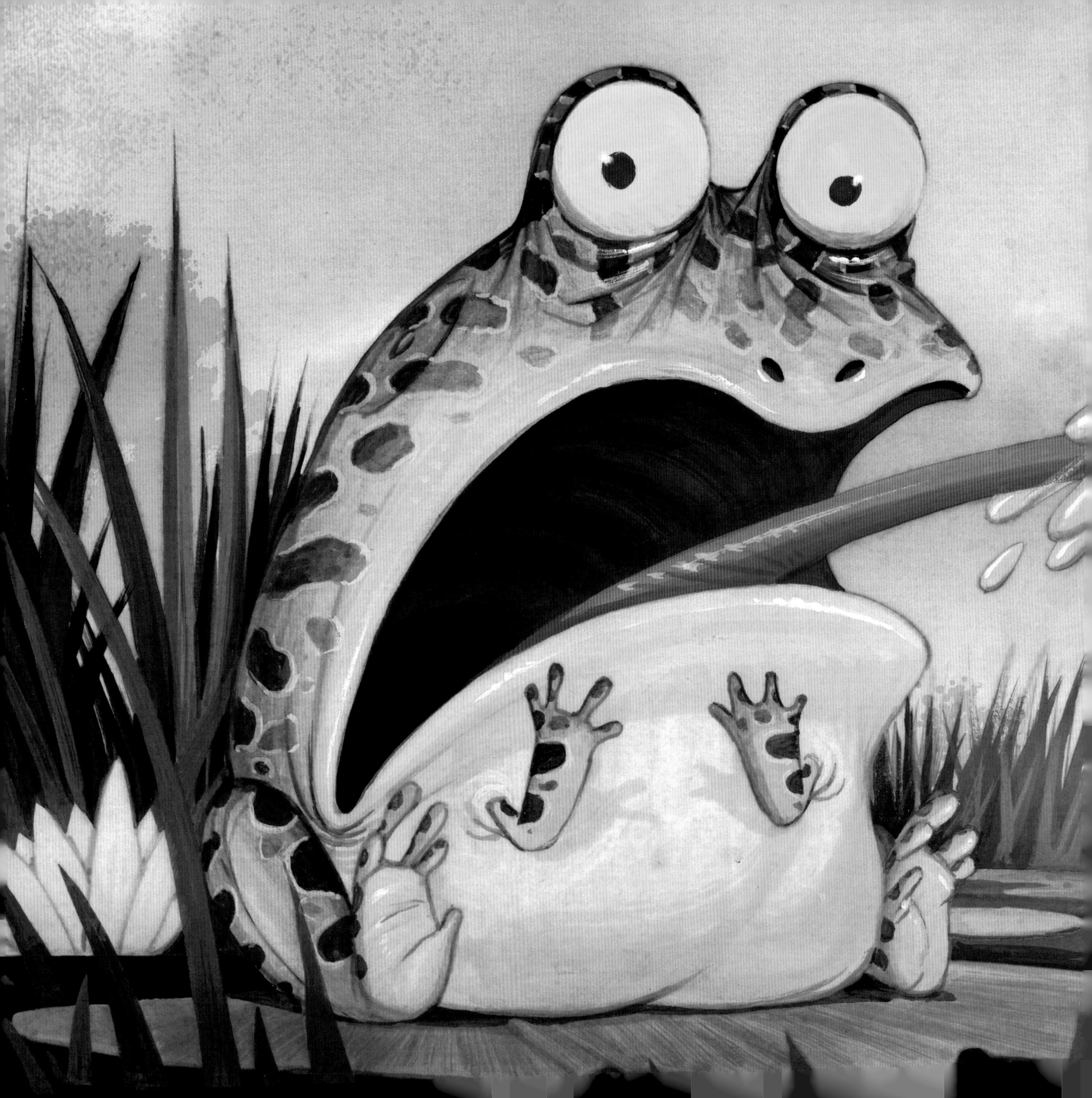

Fighting crime, slinging slime.
Save mosquitoes just in time.

Cricket choir, stage on fire.
Ants and termites — lift them higher.

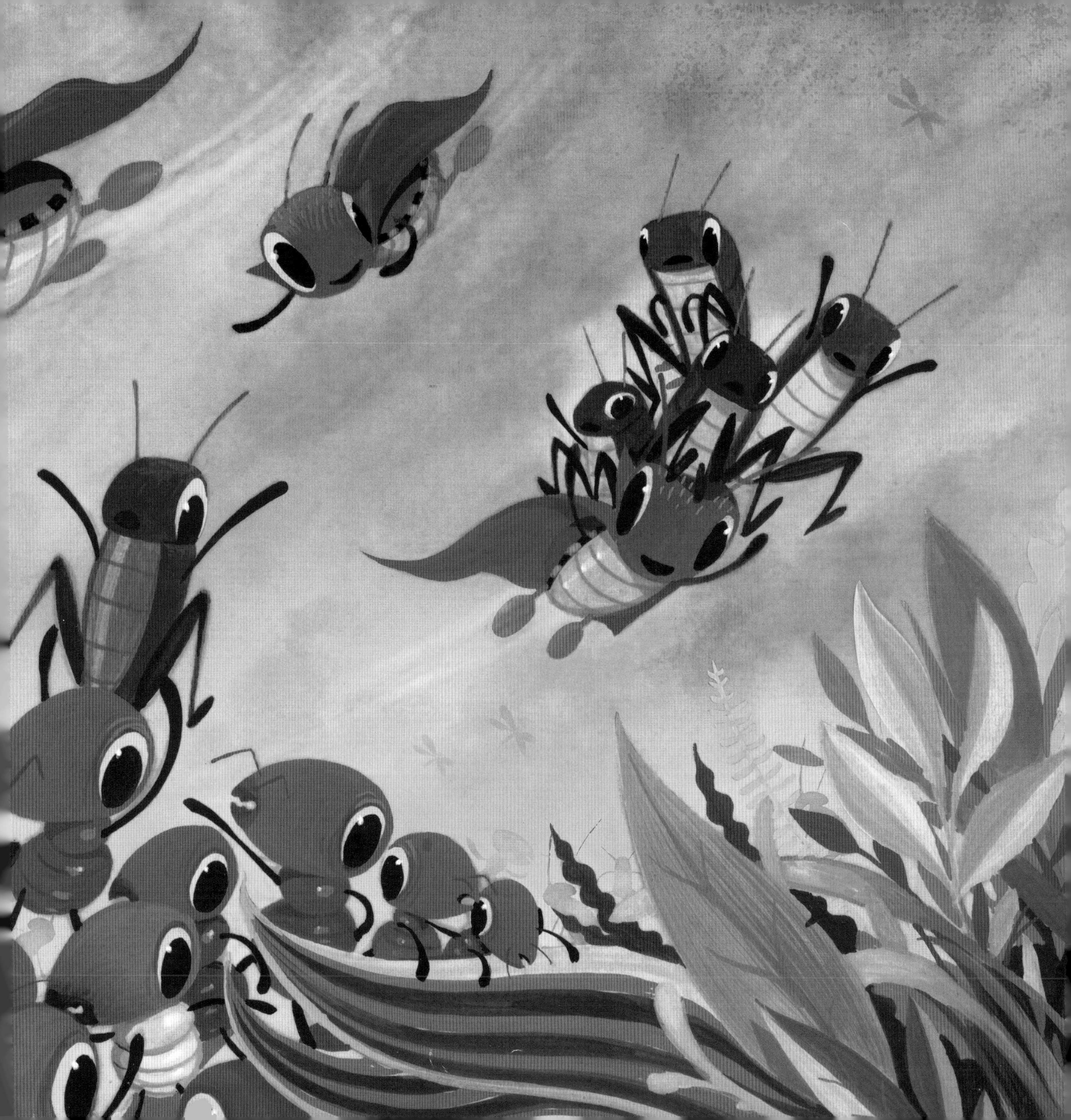

Antennae up, eyes down.
Buzzing all around the town.

Super Bugs, Super Bugs,
mighty, mighty Super Bugs!

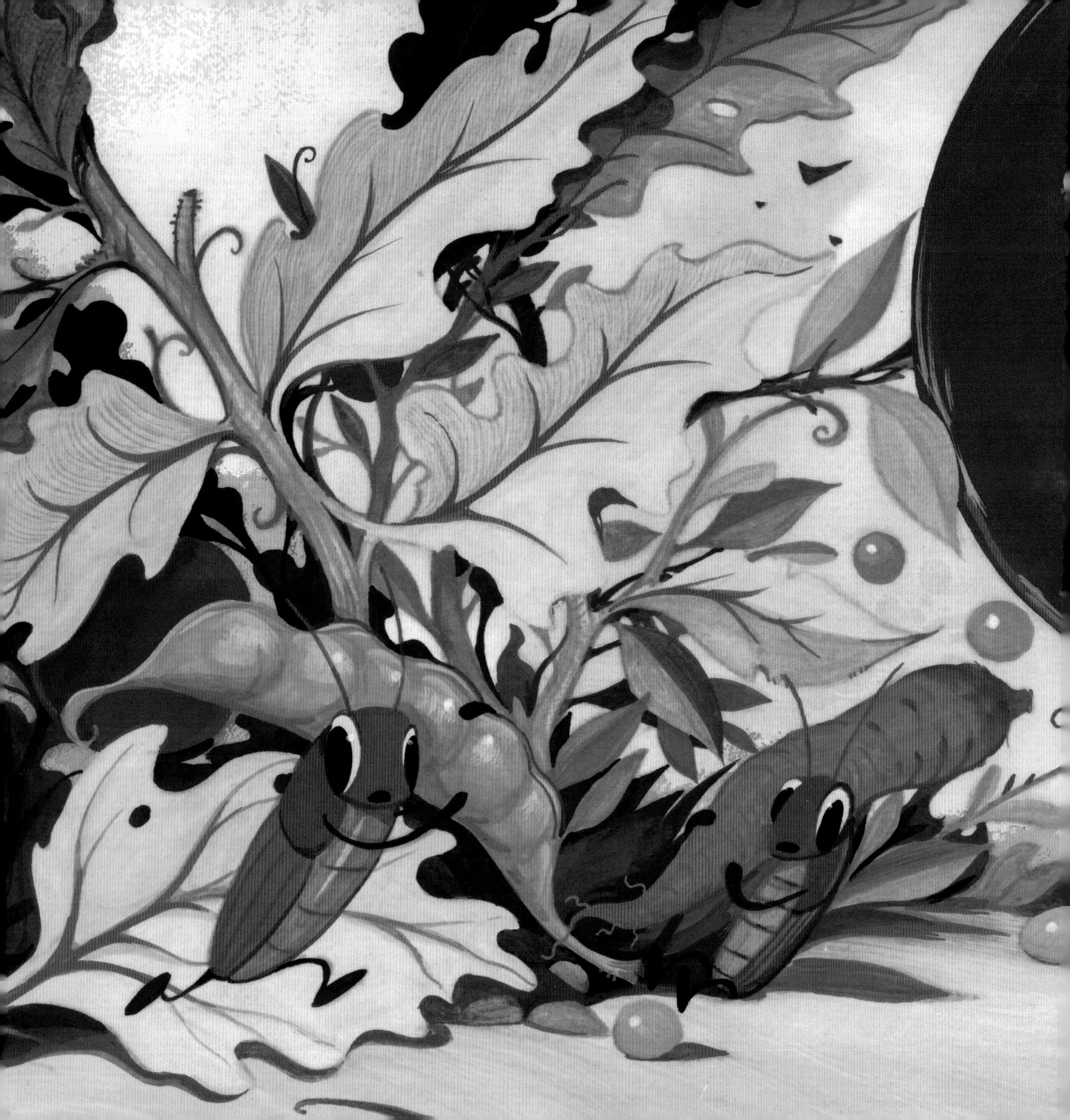

Insect shopper, green grasshopper.
Save her from a whopper bopper.

Insect coaches, rowdy roaches.
Watch out — human foot approaches.

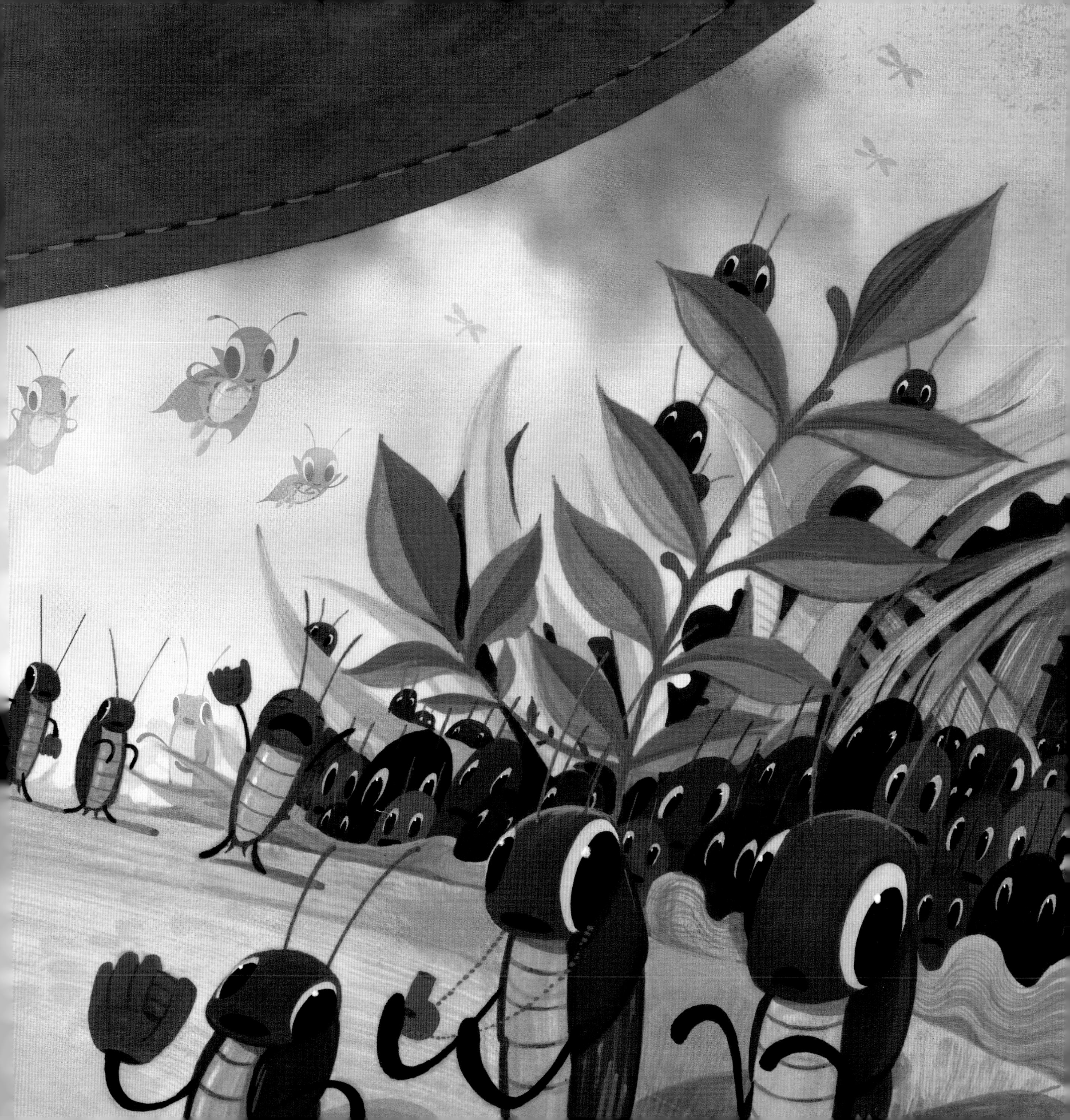

Beetles cheer, never fear.

Super Bugs are always near.

Flies and fleas, bumblebees.

Cicadas cheering from the trees.

Antennae up, eyes down.
Buzzing all around the town.

Super Bugs, Super Bugs,
mighty, mighty Super Bugs!

Superheroes save the day.

All the insects shout, "Hooray!"

**Caterpillars, butterflies,
spiders, moths, and dragonflies.**

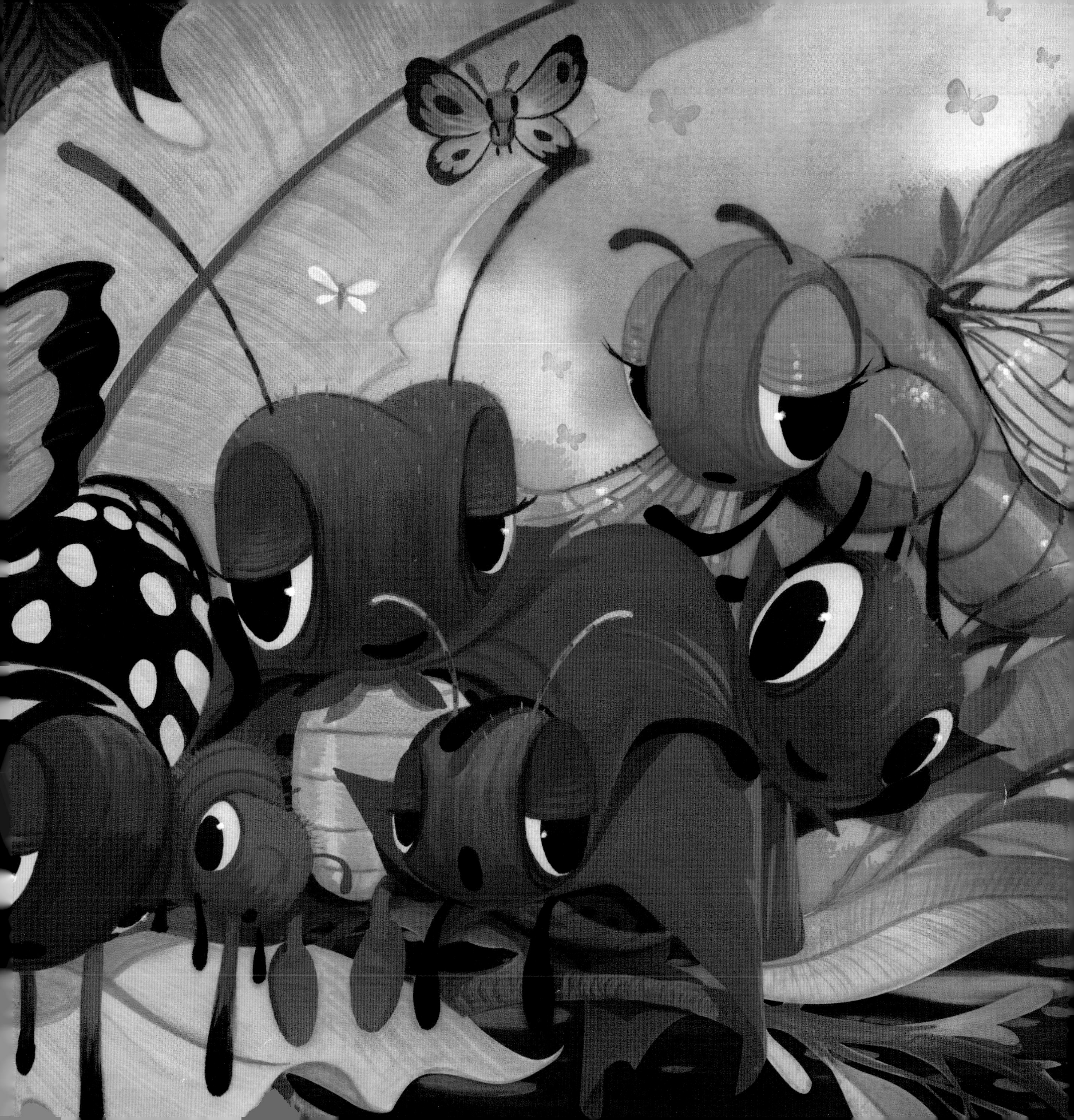

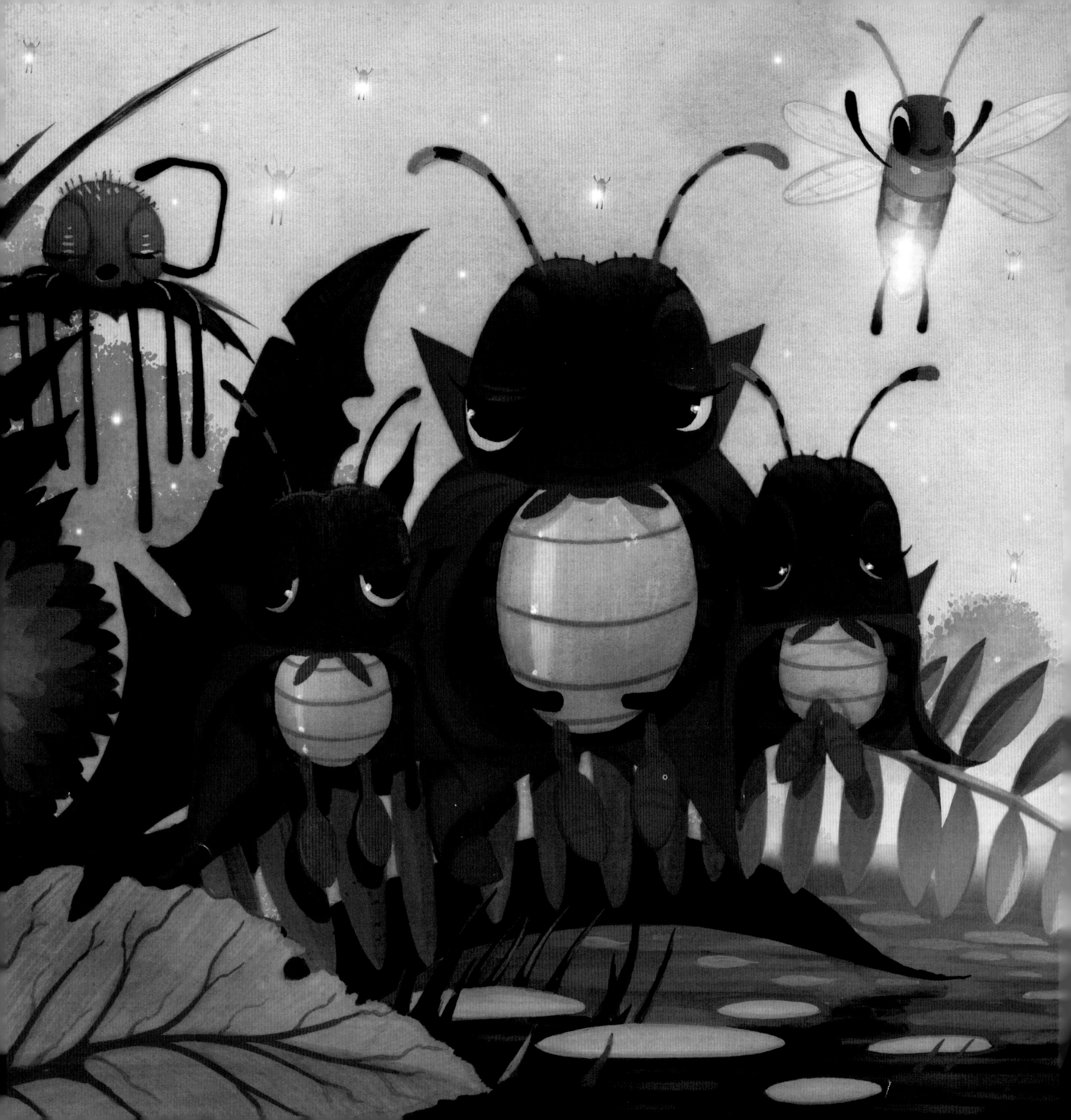

Daddy longlegs, sleepy eyes.
Fireflies are on the rise.

To the hideout — cozy nest.
Even heroes need to rest.

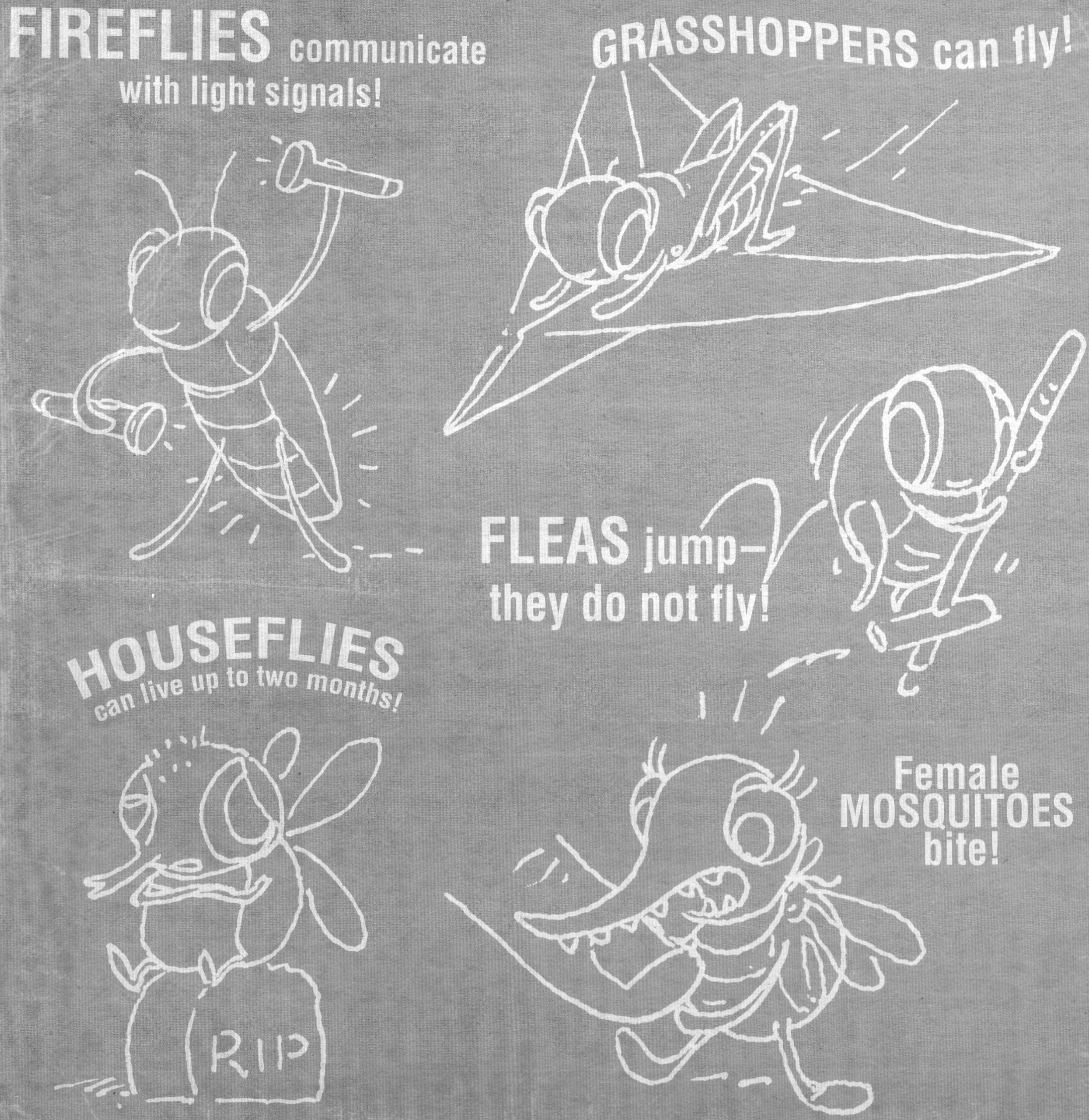
FIREFLIES communicate with light signals!
GRASSHOPPERS can fly!
FLEAS jump—they do not fly!
HOUSEFLIES can live up to two months!
RIP
Female MOSQUITOES bite!